A TALE OF SCARS AND REBELS

ALEX CLIFFORD

A TALE OF SCARS AND REBELS

A WITCHES OF WYLDEDEN NOVELLA

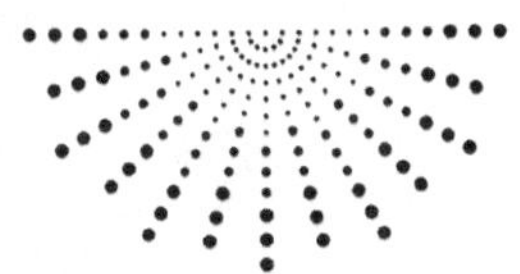

ALEX CLIFFORD

Nir
Ahrenhale
QIRI
North Mountains
Northern Spine
The Vein
Pirevia
ERVEDA
VERTLYN
Womb
Heart Lake
ysarn
Soul Lake
Orhn
ANFAR
eppa
Southern Spine
Wyldeden
Dividing River
BERNT
Hyrsch
Belden
OFORD

Northern Mountains
The Vein
Faerie Circle
Pirevia
The Strait

AIRBREAKER

OWEN

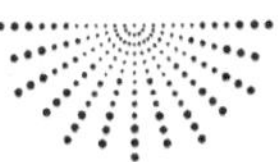

THE ONLY CONSISTENT THING ABOUT THE VOYAGE NORTH WAS the waterlogged state of Owen's boots. Access to food and fresh water was not reliable, nor was the temperament of the sea. The *Airbreaker* had begun to leak during a violent storm in the ship's first week abroad, and while being part kinner kept the trench foot at bay it did nothing to stave off the cold or hunger.

The brig in the bowels of the ship was cramped with stinking demi-kin rebels, kept in cage-like cells that were stifling during the day, yet freezing at night.

It was when the nights finally warmed that they knew it was time.

"Good luck," Owen said to Tomson, sullen in his cell across the narrow walkway.

"And to you," Tomson answered with a terse nod.

Through the wooden bars that separated him from Nora, Owen glared at his wife. Her hair was growing in black patches across her scarred scalp, as was Owen's beard, matted and reeking of vomit from the seasickness plaguing them.

"Traitor," Nora started.

"Me?" he growled, raising his voice to be heard above the creaking boards of the ship around them. "You chose a murderer, a torturer, over your own kind!"

"I've said a thousand times now that what Aisling does is in the best interest of *all* people! Not just ours, or hers, but all!"

"She sent you away on a slave ship and you're still defending her!"

"Only because you're a gods-damned liar! And for what?" Nora spat back.

Whether her fists were shaking from fury or nerves, Owen couldn't tell. The argument wasn't entirely staged, though it was hardly the first time they'd had some version of it over the past few weeks at sea.

"Quiet down there!" one of the slavers shouted from the stairwell.

"For the life of an innocent child," Owen snapped, ignoring the warning. "An innocent boy you let your precious princess torture for two years!"

"Oh, don't act so righteous. You knew he was down there, too."

"I said, shut it!" The footsteps of the slaver thumped loudly on the creaky stairs as he descended into the brig.

So much of this plan depended on sheer luck. That their cages would be close enough to the stairwell to garner the attention of the slavers, that they would be able to tell when it was time to do so, that they would be in any kind of shape to launch an escape. Owen didn't like it, but there was little choice;

Nora had not been given the luxury of consulting him when she'd hatched this insanity with Aisling.

The human man who prowled down the aisle looking for the source of the noise was a regular presence in the brig. Whether the secrecy was intentional remained unknown, but none of the sailors or slavers names had been spoken in front of the demi-kin, so they had collectively decided to nickname this one "Tongues."

"The difference is," Owen continued to argue with Nora, "that I didn't know where in the palace he was being kept. If I had, I would have helped the rebels free him sooner. But you? You knew everything going on in that palace and—"

"If I have to say it again," the slaver shouted as his boots splashed in the ankle-deep water, "I will cut out your tongues! Not worth any less to Prince Nevan without them!"

Nora ignored the slaver and his repetitive threats, hissing at Owen through teeth bared in rage. "Exactly. I know what's going on in that palace better than you do, and so I made the hard call to let Aisling do what she thought she had to do."

"That you neglected to share that information with me makes you just as much a liar as I," Owen retorted, forcing himself not to look to the slaver now approaching their cells.

"That you would have turned it over to the rebels proves I was right not to!"

"That's it." Tongues pulled a rusty dagger from his belt and went to Nora's cell, as they suspected he would. Despite her strong frame and scarred face, he assumed because she was female she was the easier target.

Fitting the key hanging around his neck into the lock, Tongues pulled the door open with more force than necessary, letting it bang loudly against the neighboring bars.

As if she had only now noticed him, Nora turned her back to Owen and gasped. "Wait, no, I'm sorry."

"Those your last words, sweet cheeks?" Tongues chuckled as he slid the blade along his own jawline.

Nora whimpered and huddled against the bars in a rather convincing display of terror. Every single demi-kin in the brig, including Owen, stayed utterly still as the slaver approached her. Silent as he stepped within range.

No matter how angry he was with her, Owen was still proud of the way Nora struck forward, quick as an asp, and clutched the slaver's wrist. A sharp twist made him drop the knife before she ducked under his arm. Twisting the wrist farther, the slaver was forced to turn, and Nora shoved him into the bars dividing her and Owen with every ounce of depleted strength in her starving body.

Owen was waiting. As the slaver's back hit, he slipped an arm between the bars and around the man's neck, pulling tight.

Nora backed off as the man clawed uselessly at Owen's arm, long scratches merely inconvenient as they decorated his skin. It had been a long time since a human had been strong enough to fight Owen off, and today was no different.

"Son of a—" Tongues ran out of breath to finish cursing, struggling like a cat caught by the tail.

It only took a few minutes for the slaver to slacken against the bars. Still, Owen waited until Nora nodded to let him go. Tongues splashed face down into the shallow water where Nora stripped him of weapons and keys. The latter she tossed to Owen so he could free himself.

None of the other prisoners asked him to unlock their cages, but every single one placed their hands against their chests, four fingers raised on one and three on the other. A salute to the seven-pointed star.

During the weeks of travel, Nora's plan had spread through the ranks and even the most hateful among them was willing to put aside their grudges to make it happen. To play a hand in the fall of Pirevia.

Owen knew most of them personally, either from the royal army or the rebellion. None resented him for choosing his family over joining them in the City of Blood. Or, if they did, they didn't voice it.

Without another word between them, Owen strapped the slaver's sword to his hip while Nora locked an unconscious Tongues in her cell. Sloshing through the water, they crept up the stairs into the mid-level where supplies were stored. Stomach aching hollowly, Owen grabbed a soft apple and took a large bite before passing it to Nora. There wasn't time to feast, but they would need whatever strength they could get.

Once on the dry landing, their boots squelched with every step, so with little more than a glance to agree, they shucked them off and left them on the stairwell. Moving quickly and quietly, they reached the ladder that would take them above deck and eased open the hatch.

Owen peered out and swore.

The ship was aglow with starlight, and while there were not many sailors awake at this time of night, he and Nora would not be able to get a rowboat into the water without the cloak of darkness.

"We'll do without the boat," Nora whispered, the bright night peeking under the hatch illuminating a strip of her face. "Orhn should not be too far to swim."

A risky guess, judged only by the change in temperature;

summer did not quite permeate the nights in Oford, but by Orhn the heat was more lasting. For all they knew, the island could be miles away still. Not to mention that neither of them had experience swimming long distances.

Again, Owen didn't think they had much choice.

They waited until the sailors began a shanty before creeping onto the deck, hoping the sound of song would cover any noise they might make. The night was by far the stillest in all the weeks they'd been at sea, which was both a blessing and a curse. Swimming would be easier, but they would also be easier to spot from the ship.

Moving like wraiths, they made a quick dash to the side of the ship. Nora slipped over silently, but the splash as she hit the water was anything but.

"What was that?" someone called.

Wincing, Owen didn't look back as he vaulted over the railing.

MER

OWEN

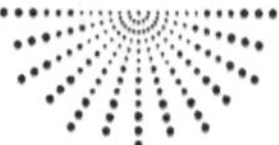

"PRISONERS OVERBOARD!"

He heard the shout just before hitting the water.

The hard surface of the sea battered his body, forcing the breath from his lungs. The heavy steel at his hip was a mistake, the weight of the weapon dragging him into the black depths of the strait. Panicked, Owen wrestled with the loop keeping the short sword to his belt until it pulled free, sinking quickly to the sea floor somewhere far below. His descent slowed, mouth and nose full of frigid salt water.

Nora was nowhere in sight.

Water rippled around him as something heavy fell from above. A rowboat, most likely, for the humans coming after them.

Ahead, the silhouette of a person swimming in his direction distinguished itself from the murky depths. He'd never reach them without a fresh breath.

As smoothly as he could, Owen swam for the surface, and as

his head breached, he decided he was grateful for the still night after all. Not too far in the distance he could see the island of Orhn—a stretch of shadow against the blanket of bright stars mirrored in the black water.

Before enacting this insane plan, Nora had arranged for a small boat to meet them there. Any farther north and the sea became a cesspool of beasts and fae, but the water southward was too rough to swim through.

This was their only shot.

As he'd suspected, a rowboat had been pushed off the *Airbreaker*, two sailors onboard, paddling aimlessly. With the water utterly still and the night clear, the stars were perfectly reflected on the black water and the sailors couldn't orient themselves in the dazzling seascape. As long as Owen didn't make any sudden movements, he should be able to avoid their attention.

The water around his legs stirred, and he looked down expecting Nora to have found him. A shadow beneath the surface had stopped inches away. Two of the stars reflected in the water blinked.

"Oh, f—"

Hands like steel grabbed his legs and yanked him beneath the surface.

Down, down, down.

A look at the creature holding his ankles almost made him scream. Bluish skin, seaweed hair, and a long tail that glittered copper under the starlight—he'd never seen the merfolk before, and he didn't want to be seeing them now.

Shouldn't be seeing them now. Not this far south.

Shaking a leg free, he kicked the sea beast. Its delicate bones snapped beneath his foot and the violent screech the creature made was piercing, even under water. Gills flaring, it gnashed razor teeth as it let go of his other foot.

More dark shapes were rushing up from below. Owen was moments away from becoming dinner.

Kicking back to the surface and taking a deep breath, he desperately searched for Nora.

Had the mer gotten her?

Grief strangled his throat at the thought.

The splashing and shouting of the sailors as they rowed toward him forced Owen to focus. Treading water wasn't going to save Nora.

"Merfolk!" he called out as he swam toward the sailors, saltwater burning his cracked lips.

"You damned fool! Get in the boat!"

Cold hands wrapped around his ankles again as he scrambled onto the vessel, splinters digging beneath his nails as he grabbed hold of the bench seat and yanked hard. The boat rocked, sending the standing sailors stumbling. Before they could right themselves, Owen hauled himself up and shoved the largest one overboard.

The water churned frenziedly, the man's scream swallowed by the sea as mer began to feast.

"You shit!" The second sailor lunged for Owen, knife drawn.

Owen threw his weight to rock the boat again. Cussing loudly, the sailor dropped the knife to grab the edge of the boat, but it didn't save him as Owen kicked out his knee. Toppling over the side, the second sailor splashed into the churning water.

"Nora!" Owen called into the night, not ready to give up on her.

Another rowboat dropped into the sea, three more men

onboard. It didn't matter that his shouts got their attention; there was no way they'd missed the screams of their crew.

"Over here!" Nora's rasping voice called.

Barely visible in the ship's shadow, Nora clung to the anchor's chain with her feet pulled up, merfolk scrambling over each other to get at her.

A shudder of undiluted terror ran down his spine as Owen grabbed the oars and pushed them through the floating chunks of men in the water.

Realizing what he was doing, the men in the other rowboat turned toward Nora too, much closer than Owen. The merfolk noticed their approach and dove beneath the surface so smoothly it was as if they'd never been there at all.

A nervous hush quieted the sailors as they neared the anchor, the sudden stillness more worrying than Owen's frantic rowing in their direction. One reached for Nora's foot while the other two kept eyes on the water, but they were still taken off guard as moon-pale hands shot up and grabbed the side of the boat, pulling it onto its side. The sailors had knives at the ready, stabbing at the shimmery hands of the sea beasts. Blood sprayed over the humans' faces, but the mer barely noticed their wounds as they capsized the boat.

Weapons made of steel might injure, but they wouldn't deter a beast. It was why Owen's own military weapons had been part silver—weapons he would have sold his soul for right then.

Ignoring the strangled cries beside him, Owen pulled his boat alongside the ship. Nora dropped in, wheezing and shaking and, without a word, took one of the oars and started counting. In tandem, they steered toward the island.

"I didn't think there were mer this far south," Owen panted, shoulders already burning as the lack of exercise these past weeks caught up with him.

Nora shook her head. "Me neither. You okay?"

"Oh yeah, just swell."

A loud *cha-clunk* echoed through the night, followed by a long whistle.

"Down!" Owen shouted, ducking low.

From the enormous crossbow mounted on the ship's bow, a bolt as long as his arm pierced right through Nora's oar, shattering it into splinters.

"Move," he said, shuffling past Nora to stand at the stern of the boat with a two-handed grip on his oar. Breathing through the strain in his weakened muscles, limbs shaking from exertion, he continued rowing. He wanted to be out of range before the sailors had time to reload the crossbow.

A sharp tug on the oar broke his momentum, almost sending him sprawling as he struggled to hold onto it. Roaring with frustration, Nora grabbed a hold of Owen's shoulder, half to steady him and half to balance herself as she peered over the edge and aimed a kick for the merfolk's face.

Cha-clunk.

Owen hit the deck, dragging Nora with him as the bolt shot over their heads.

He'd dropped the second oar.

"Damn it!" Nora's voice cracked as she scrambled for it, but it was already lost to the black depths.

"We got this," Owen said, the words automatic. "We got this."

Looking around, he wasn't sure how, exactly, they had this.

Another splash. A third rowboat.

"We've got to swim," Nora said, shaking as she turned toward the *Airbreaker*.

"We can't."

"I'm not getting back on that ship, Owen. There won't be another chance. We'll go to Pirevia. Siobhan . . ." Her sentence deteriorated into stuttering, hand resting on her stomach.

Pale hands shot out of the water and grabbed the edge of their boat. Nora struck forward, screaming in rage as she lashed out with clenched fists. The crack of brittle bones heralded a pained screech as the mer retracted its hand.

"Stay in the boat," Owen said.

He had an idea. A stupid idea, but not any more insane than this plan had been to begin with. Rolling his shoulders, he slipped over the edge and into the sea.

"No! Owen!"

White knuckled grip on the boat, shivering from the cold, he kicked the mer that reached for him.

"What are you doing, you fucking idiot!"

Ignoring her screams, he shimmied his way to the stern and began kicking. Pushing. He had little control over the direction they were going, but at least they were moving.

The water rippled as the mer returned for him. Owen stopped to bat it away but missed. The sea-beast's teeth bit into his calf before darting away.

"We got this," he chanted, ignoring the flash of pain in his leg as he resumed swimming. "We got this."

"You're insane. You are an insane person, Owen. Do you know that?" Nora cried, even as she beat at the pale hands reaching over the lip of their boat.

Cha-clunk.

A heavy splash close by. The slavers on the ship couldn't see them anymore apparently, but the rowboat was still chasing them. If Owen could just get to Orhn, there would be supplies waiting. Weapons. On land, they could fight.

Numbness crept up his leg. He stopped being able to kick.

"Oh, damn it all!" he cussed, spitting out sea water.

"What? What? What's wrong? What?"

The boat slowed as his leg failed.

"Help me," he said as he hauled himself up.

Nora counterbalanced the boat while reaching for his arm, anchoring him as he crawled back in. Sweeping his gaze over the horizon, he couldn't even see the island anymore.

Nora's hands searched his body, shaking so hard that when she found the punctures on his calf her fingers nearly tore them open. Hissing, she pulled back.

"Apparently mer are venomous," he panted.

They sat for a moment with only the steady splashing of oars in the distance breaking the silence. That, and the single sob Nora let herself have before standing up.

"Over here!" she called. "We surrender! Over here!"

"Nora!" Owen hissed, pulling her back down.

"Escaping is pointless if you die," she said, voice breaking again. "When we get back to Siobhan, we will arrive together. Alive. Both of us."

Closing his eyes, Owen held back a sigh of defeat. The numbness was spreading. He would heal faster than most humans, but not if the venom stilled his heart first.

As the rowboat approached, the slaver with his short swords drawn looked inclined to gut them both right there and then.

"We surrender," Nora repeated, hands raised.

Owen bit his tongue, contemplating the likelihood of being able to get rid of all three men and take their oars. But the numbness was up to his waist now. He needed to stay as still as he could to stop the venom from killing him.

As the men pulled alongside them, one of the rowers stood back and took in Owen's injured leg.

"You two are in so much shit."

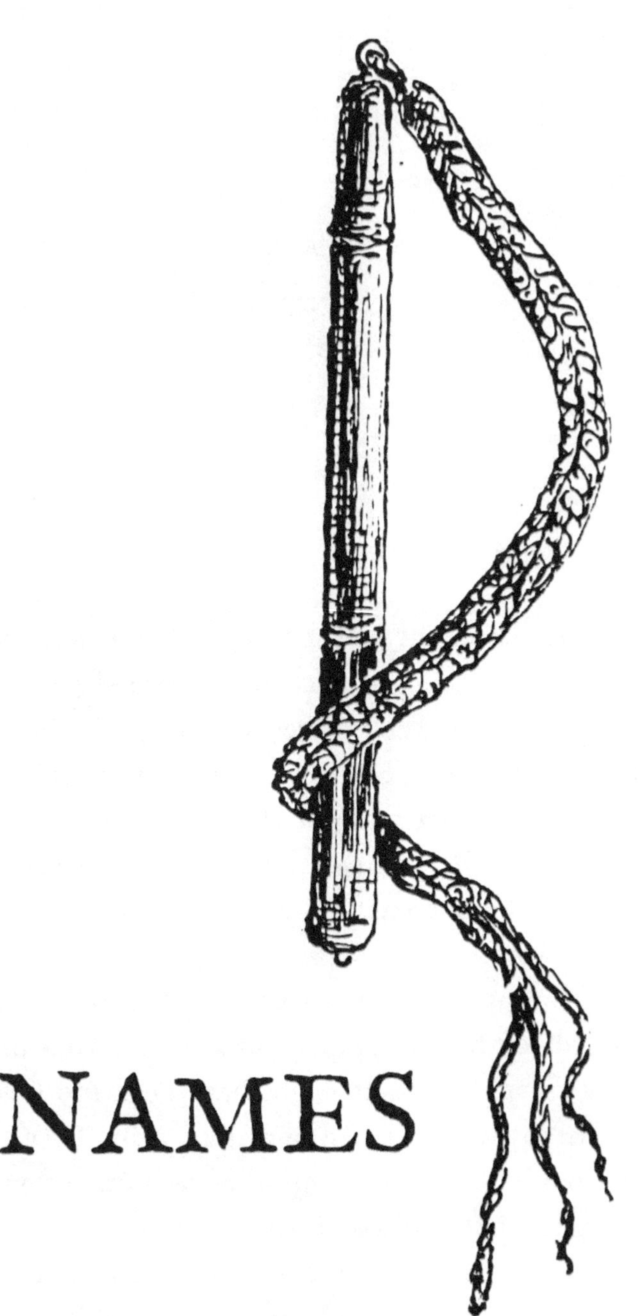

NAMES

NORA

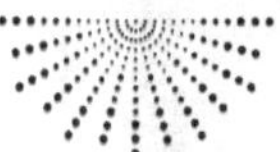

THE AIR WAS THICK WITH COLLECTIVE DISAPPOINTMENT AS Nora and Owen were dragged back down into the brig. The demi-kin still locked in their cages didn't speak, but their lowered chins and eyes spoke of their regret. Nora didn't have room for those feelings; she was just glad not to be on the deck anymore, her back still burning. Glad that the slaver called Tongues had still been unconscious, and that punishment didn't include anything worse than a whipping.

Though the whipping had been brutal. Men had died, and each of those still left had taken their turn tearing strips of flesh from hers and Owen's backs. It might have been too much to bear, but neither of them were strangers to pain. They'd kept their gazes locked on each other, acting as each other's anchors through the air-splitting cracks of leather on flesh.

Tossed back in their cells, Nora grit her teeth as salt water splashed against her raw back. Her shirt was tossed in after her, but not her boots. Too slow to grab it, her shirt fluttered into the pool of water at the bottom of her cell and was immediately soaked through.

Only after the slavers left did Owen let himself cuss. Colorfully.

"What happened?" Tomson asked, standing at the bars of his cell, fists wrapped tight around the wood.

"Merfolk," Nora answered, knowing Owen was beyond words right now as he slammed his fist into the water. Her voice shook as she put herself in the least awful position she could find, breathing deeply. It would take days to heal, but she would heal. There would be no infection, but there would be scars. It had been a long time since she'd had fresh ones.

The other demi-kin took the hint that neither of them were in the mood for discussing what had gone wrong. One of the soldiers, Luna, began to hum softly just to fill the quiet, lulling them to a fitful sleep.

With only the sound of the waves crashing against the hull, Nora and Owen sat as close as they could, hands intertwined between the bars separating them.

"I'm sorry," Nora said again. She'd said it a thousand times, but as the days went by and they grew closer to Pirevia, Owen withdrew deeper into his own head.

"It's my fault," he answered, brow furrowing. "If I'd buried the bodies instead of tossing them in the river, we wouldn't be here."

That was the only problem he had with what he'd done, she knew. Not that he had killed soldiers, other demi-kin. Not that he had betrayed Aisling. Just that he'd been caught. One day, they would need to have another conversation about that, but she was too tired now. There wasn't much time left before they would be thrown into the thick of things, facing whatever nightmares Pirevia had to offer.

Despite their fighting, she loved him. And he loved her. Whatever time they still had, she wanted to spend it in peace.

"I like Shawn," she said. At his deepening frown, she clarified where her train of thought had gone. "If the baby is a boy. I like the name Shawn."

Owen shuddered, practically gagging, though whether that was due to the seasickness that still plagued him, she didn't know. "There was a Shawn in my dorm when I was in the cadets. Really bad gas."

"That's not because his name was Shawn." Nora raised her eyebrows, resting her forehead against the bars between them.

Resting his own against hers, Owen seemed grateful for the distraction. "What about Damien?"

"After the smuggler?"

"I already took his last name, but I will never . . . I owe him everything."

The urge to apologize again almost overwhelmed her. Owen had told his story many years ago. Damien Turlough had gone down into the prison aptly named "the sewers" looking for one particular demi-kin, ignoring the curses spat by those he left behind. But Owen's mother had not sworn or begged. She had been silent, holding seven-year-old Owen against her. For some reason, her stillness had caught the smuggler's attention. It was the defining moment of Owen's life. The moment Damien had turned his gaze from the silent woman, crouched down in front of Owen, and asked, *Can you be quiet?*

"Damien is a good name." Nora reached across to smooth

the beard growing across his jawline. "What about for a girl? And don't say Siobhan."

Owen managed a fond smile. "Why? It would be nice after what she's done for us."

Yes, he no doubt had less reservations about their surrogate than she did. It wasn't him that Siobhan had lied so thoroughly to.

"Because I immediately think of all the scheming and all our fighting about it, and I don't want any of that associated with the baby."

His smile turned chagrined as he nodded. "Well, we're not calling her Aisling, either."

Scoffing, Nora pinched his ear. It had never crossed her mind. Despite her own reverence for the princess of Hyrsch, it had become abundantly clear that Owen had never truly trusted her.

Taking Nora's hand from his ear, Owen held it against his cheek and leaned into the touch. She sighed, relishing the warmth of him. Their backs had become a latticework of pink, shiny lines, and being unable to take advantage of their quick healing by curling up together was practically a second punishment.

Thinking of her scars, she said, "For a girl . . . my mother's name was Lesley."

Just as Owen had told her about his life, Nora had told him of hers.

Lesley was born and died a slave. She'd hidden her pregnancy, then hidden Nora in the attic of their master's house for years, but it hadn't been enough. She'd been discovered, and though Lesley had tried everything to protect her daughter, the scars all over Nora's body said enough as to why, even before Hyrsch had been free, the city had been safer than the privacy of that country house.

Getting her daughter out had cost Lesley's life. There was no grave that Nora knew of, no memorial of her mother's sacrifice anywhere. But a daughter of her own . . .

Owen nodded. "Lesley or Damien."

The two of them sat, shivering in the leaking brig. At least Siobhan was safe. No matter how cross Nora was with the human woman, she was glad for that. With a sniff, she squeezed Owen's hand.

"If I don't make it, promise me you will find Siobhan."

"Don't talk like that," Owen scolded, throat bobbing madly at her words.

She understood, and though she was confident in this plan, she still pleaded. "Promise me, Owen."

"Only if you do."

She imagined it then. Taking the city from Prince Nevan but finding out Owen hadn't survived. The immediate burning in her throat rivaled that which had scorched her back earlier. Then, finding Siobhan and telling her the baby would never know their father. Raising the child for years, missing him at every milestone.

No scar on her flesh would run as deep as that one would. But she nodded anyway, the grip they had on each other tightening as the swell of the sea rocked them once again.

PIREVIA

OWEN

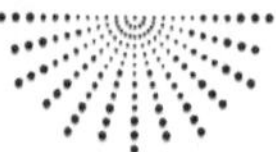

THE ONLY THING OWEN REMEMBERED ABOUT THE SEVEN YEARS he spent growing up in Pirevia was the dark, so as he was pulled from the *Airbreaker* and assaulted by the bright sun, it was like seeing the city for the first time.

Gulls cawed from the cloudless sky, the white of their feathers like mud compared to the glistening sandstone of the palace towers. From the dock, the corroded cliff lifting the city and its surrounding swampland out of reach of the hungry sea meant a neck-breaking staircase had been built to bring sailors and fishermen into Pirevia.

The human men and women shouting at one another as they offloaded their hauls dimmed as the first demi-kin prisoners descended the ramp onto the docks.

Between the stink of gutted tuna and the creeping scent of blood and refuse that started Owen's mind tumbling back into itself, the urge to cause a scene, to give the slavers no choice but to kill him before he had to face this city, was overwhelming.

A heaviness pressed down on the back of his head as his chains dragged over the wooden planks, echoed by the dozens of others in front and behind. Nora turned, pity in her eyes. On the journey, Owen had told her and the others all he remembered about this place so they would be prepared, trying not to let the festering fear in his gut show, but Nora knew. Since the moment they met, she had always known what ate at him from within.

Giving her a soft nod of assurance, Owen forced himself to raise his chin. There was no room for weakness in Pirevia.

At the end of the dock stood a warehouse, paint faded from sea spray but otherwise in better condition than the other buildings along the cliff's base. The prisoners were ushered over the threshold, the shade a relief from the brutal sun, and it quickly became clear why this building was in such good condition.

Rhosyn Shaye, consort of Prince Nevan, stood in her finery with a small battalion's worth of blue-and-gold clad guards. She held a handkerchief against her delicate nose, but her bright blue eyes scanned every face as they came to stand in a line.

The network of Hyrschan spies, both rebel and royal, had confirmed the rumor that Rhosyn met every shipment of demi-kin personally, looking for someone. The disappointment on her face became more pronounced as she paced the line, and when none were who she wanted, she fetched a velvet sack of coins from her pocket and handed it to the captain.

With a low bow, he and his men left. Tongues spat at Nora's bare feet as he passed.

Rhosyn spoke quietly to her guards before she, too, left with half a dozen of them.

The remaining guards went to heavy sacks stacked along the wall and pulled metal collars from within, hands on hilts as they waited for the demi-kin to fight against the placement of the steel around their necks. Their stillness, brimming with silent hatred, was almost as unsettling as the familiar tingle of magic that raised the hair on the back of Owen's neck as the collar locked into place.

A crease growing between the guards' brows was the only sign of their wariness at the demi-kins unprecedented level of complicity. One particular guard stepped forward, wearing slightly more gold armor than the rest, and, starting at the head of the line, gave each demi-kin a quick appraisal followed by a sharp bark in a foreign language Owen didn't understand. Probably Kerv, from the homeland of the Sparrows.

It didn't matter that the words were foreign; Owen knew what the witches were deciding. There were only three places in Pirevia for demi-kin: the arena, the sewers, or the factory. The first was Prince Nevan's infamous source of entertainment for the bloodthirsty citizens of his city, and though Owen didn't know exactly what went on there, he knew it was the best of the three options. The sewers . . . He couldn't go back down there. He'd lose his mind. And the factory was where demi-kin went for punishment. As if their lives weren't enough so already. Born in the sewers, Owen had seen plenty of demi-kin hauled away to the factory. They came back as mince down the feeding troughs.

As the golden-clad witch spoke, the other guards began separating the new slaves into three groups.

When it was Owen's turn, he looked the witch in the eye and clenched his fists.

"*Vestiko*," the guard decided, oblivious to Owen's simmering rage.

He let himself be grabbed by the elbow and moved into a

group beside Tomson. Then he watched, stomach hollow, as the guard stood in front of Nora.

"*Ostikov*," he said.

Flexing his hands, Owen shut his eyes and loosed a shaky breath. It wasn't as if being separated was new for him and Nora, but that had been Hyrsch. This place was different.

Settling the rising panic, he forced himself to open his eyes again. If everything went smoothly, this could be the last time he saw Nora for a while. If things went wrong, it could be the last time he saw her at all.

Hooded and crammed in the back of a prison wagon, Owen bided his time. The horse-drawn cart rattled over sticky cobblestone roads while civilians shamelessly placed bets on which of the demi-kin would end up in the arena.

The arena.

He had guessed it was where he would end up. A part of him was relieved not to be going back underground, even if meant there was a larger chance of Nora going there. Once, the arena had been his only chance of getting out. Once, he would have felt privileged to be taken there.

Eventually, the chatter of the crowd died off. Large metal gates screeched and clanged, over and over as the cart was pulled through layers of security. When they finally stopped, Owen was yanked out of the prison cart, shoved into open air, and freed of his hood.

The demi-kin selected for the arena stood in the center of a flat dirt ring, divots the size of boulders riddling the ground. A stone wall three men high surrounded them, and beyond that lay rows upon rows of seats, disrupted only by the royal box—a raised platform with a shade cloth pulled taut above a luxurious settee.

Three gates were set into the curved wall, two barred and locked with spellmarks while the one directly behind the wagon was decorative wrought iron.

The guards wasted no time shuttling the prisoners to one of the two barred gates, unlocking it with a muttered spell and leading the demi-kin through. Owen's calves burned as he navigated the steep slope beyond the gate, the dirt hallway changing to cobbled stone and intermittently lit by thick candles in glass lanterns. The familiar smell of filthy bodies grew stronger until the hallway opened into an enormous underground dome, lined with more cells. Not many were occupied.

Owen was put in one by himself, his chains finally removed. The urge to attack almost overwhelmed him, but escaping now would only screw over the others, and he'd long outgrown the selfishness that might have abandoned them anyway. Across the holding room, Tomson had a similar expression of repressed violence twisting his face.

Without a word, the guards checked the candles in the lamps before climbing back up the steep slope toward the surface.

The silence they left behind lasted exactly two seconds.

"So, welcome to the arena," the female in the cell beside Owen's called out, unprompted. "The girl who lived there before you died yesterday."

"I don't care," Owen answered, inspecting his cell.

Clean would be overstating things, but compared to the ship, compared to the sewers, the stale hay on the floor and refuse bucket in the corner were luxuries. The lock on his cell wasn't the standard tumble-and-key type either, which was frustrating but planned for.

"If you win, they feed you," the female continued. "Not many people win."

Owen ignored her.

Not discouraged by the newcomer's silence, she shuffled closer to the bars along the front of the cells.

"I win all the time," she bragged.

"Oh, shut up, Cecelia," someone called out.

"Nobody fucking cares!" another shouted, followed by echoes of half-assed agreement.

Cecelia ignored them as effectively as Owen ignored her. "Next time I win, I'll share my food with you."

Now he was listening. "Why?"

"Because if you figure out those locks, you're gonna open mine too, yeah?"

The holding room was not large, and the curve of the wall allowed him the barest view of the prisoners beside him. Cecelia's hair was slicked back with dried mud, her face a motley of brown and yellow bruises. Scabs had swollen her lips and knuckles, but none of it dulled the feral spark behind her bloodshot eyes.

"What if I told you I was going to open all these cells?"

He hadn't said it loudly, and there hadn't been much sound to begin with, but a hush fell over the room anyway.

"Oh, really?" Cecelia raised a mocking eyebrow.

"Yeah, and when I do, you're all going to help me with something."

"Let me guess, you came up with some grand escape plan in the last hour that one of us ain't tried in all our months." She practically laughed, though it was bitter and full of bite.

"Years," someone else called out in response.

"No," Owen grumbled, slamming his hand against the lock. In the corner of his cell was a second bucket, this one filled with water. He didn't know how long it was supposed to last, so he drank frugally. "*We* came up with a plan a month ago."

Tomson hadn't wanted to risk telling the Pirevians about the plan this early, and even now from across the room, he was shaking his head in warning. One of them could be a spy, might try to sell the information to Nevan in exchange for freedom, or whatever version of it they could get in Pirevia. But Owen knew these people. Not specifically, but Pirevian demi-kin in general. Nevan would give them nothing, and they knew it. Not even a clean rag to wipe their asses. A clean death wasn't even on the cards.

These people were hungry. Hungry to see this city burn.

"A month ago," Cecelia said with wry disbelief. "You expect us to believe your stupid ass came here on purpose, with a plan to bust us all out? Our vigilante hero."

"Me." He nodded. "And the two dozen demi-kin who came with me. The fourteen Hyrschan spies who know we are here. The three hundred Hyrschan soldiers marching this way as we speak. And my wife, Second in Command to Princess Aisling Aurnia, who will be laying claim to this city by the end of summer."

Silence answered him, along with a mixture of grimaces and hopeful faces. The hope was a surprise.

"So, when I get these locks open, you going to help or what?" he asked.

Cecelia snorted. "Let's see you live that long first."

SEWERS

NORA

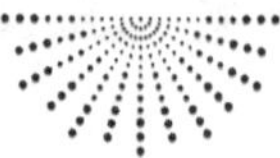

Not long after watching Owen's prison cart depart from Blood Boulevard, the one Nora was in rolled through the ornate palace gates and came to a halt. She stopped scratching at the raw patch of skin already grating beneath her collar and took in as much of her surroundings as possible. At least until the golden-clad guard stepped in the way.

"That's it, drink it in, mutts. This is the last bit of sunlight you'll be seeing before you're minced," he sneered, unlocking the wagon and hauling the nearest prisoner out.

Off to the side of the main path leading toward the white-stone palace was a bare courtyard with only a jutting structure far too small to be a prison. As rough hands pulled her from the wagon, Nora joined the others in a single file, keeping her head down and her mouth shut as the guards opened the door to the structure, revealing a wide staircase descending into blackness. The steep, blood-flecked steps were the least of her concerns as the reek of refuse and decay wafted up from the darkness, many of those before her gagging or outright vomiting.

"Do your new accommodations offend your delicate Oford sensibilities?" One of the guards pushed the rebel male who'd heaved his guts on the step.

Nora caught him by the arm before he could go crashing down the stairwell.

"Focus," she muttered.

The male bared his teeth and snatched his arm back. He was young, but by far the angriest of all the rebels onboard the *Airbreaker*, and he had not held back when Nora first explained the plan back in the brig. He had not wanted anything to do with any plan Aisling was a part of, no matter how "good" a cause it was for. Eventually the others had talked him into it, but he had never warmed to Nora.

Down they went until the hall at the bottom of the stairs branched in two. Nora could taste the filth in the air, the pungency worse to the left. There was a collective sagging among the demi-kin when the guard turned them that way, marching down a stone floor that became stickier the deeper they went.

Before Aisling had arrived, when Oford had been at its worst, Lord Hawthorn had still never kept demi-kin in conditions like this. It broke her heart knowing Owen had been born in this festering underground nightmare, fed on the promise that if he survived long enough he might be chosen for the arena. Throwing himself into whatever bloody amusements the humans dwelling in the city above concocted was the only escape from this place the Pirevians called "the sewers."

Again, the hall forked. It didn't seem to matter which way

they went this time; hoarse coughs and weary shuffling came from both directions. Turning left again, eyes burning from the urge to vomit, Nora noticed compartments lining the walls. Stone rooms with two or three glow worms trapped in broken jars to shed light upon the ravaged occupants. Not as many as Nora had thought there might be. Sometimes three, usually only two to a cell, the occupants watched the newcomers with a mixture of apathy and raw hatred.

Except the children. Their wide eyes watched with curiosity.

Nora blinked back tears as she passed them.

Without rhyme or reason, the guards began pulling demi-kin aside and shoving them into cells. The occupants of the one Nora was pushed into kept far away from the open barred door, making no attempt to escape.

With vicious looks on their faces, the male and female leaned against the wall seething. As the door clanged shut behind her, Nora returned their glare.

She had thought her clothes ruined from the long journey at sea, but they were in fine condition compared to the scraps of rags the Pirevian demi-kin wore. Along the back wall of the cell was a deep groove, its purpose unclear. A faucet with no tap dripped slowly into a wooden bowl, half full of water that, even in the limited lighting, didn't appear to be clean.

There was nowhere for waste to go. Nora tried not to think too long on that as her bare feet stuck and squelched against what should have been a stone floor.

Her new cellmates could make or break this plan, and right now she was more nervous than she'd ever been since the moment she'd suggested it to Aisling. The three of them remained frozen until the guards left, not even the echo of their boots remaining. It was the emaciated male who moved first, pushing off the wall and licking his lips as he stalked forward.

If he was trying to intimidate her, he was in for a shock. There as so little meat on his bones that Nora could have snapped him in half without ever having trained a day in her life.

"Fancy threads," he noted, voice low and scratchy.

"You too," Nora managed before gagging.

He wasn't insulted or shamed. What shame could be had when cleanliness was an utterly foreign concept? Judging by the pale shine of the pitiful light reflecting off his cheekbones, jaundiced eyes dilated from peering through the dark, he had likely lived down here his entire life.

"Oford bitch," the female hissed. Her anger suggested she might have spent some time above. Not much, judging by the similarities in their skin and eyes.

"You recognize my accent?" Nora asked.

"We've had a few up from your way before." She knew Pirevia was north of Oford, then. "They didn't last long."

"Well, I don't plan on being here long, either."

The female grinned, and before Nora could explain further, the male lunged.

It was barely an effort to send him sprawling face down in his own filth. Screeching, the female grabbed a fistful of the short hair at the base of Nora's neck, swinging a shard of glass from a broken jar. Nora blocked the blow with her forearm and burning pain sliced across her skin. Crying out, she grabbed and rotated the female's wrist until it snapped. Her scream roused the male, who grabbed Nora's ankle and bit down hard.

"Fuck!" Nora spat, kicking him in the face.

The female slashed at Nora's face again, but the broken wrist had sapped her strength and Nora was able to shove back, jabbing a fist into her throat before scrambling free from both of them.

The occupants of the cell across the hall stood at the bars, watching eagerly.

"My turn for thigh meat," one muttered, licking his cracked lips. "You promised, remember."

"Shut up," the male said, staggering to his feet and holding the side of his head where Nora's kick had broken the skin. It was not healing as fast as it should have.

"Marbled, this one, she looks like," another croaked from across the hall, words garbled as if they couldn't move their mouth properly.

A cold flush spread across Nora's skin. Owen had not mentioned this. Either he didn't remember, or things had gotten worse in the past twenty years.

"I will kill you long before you get a chance to cut me again," Nora warned her cellmates, holding her bleeding arm. It was a deep cut and would take a few hours to heal.

"She says, but her face looks like she's good at getting cut," the female cackled.

"I am Second in Command to Princess Aisling herself, trained personally by the captain of her guard. You surprised me, but it won't happen again."

"Was."

"Excuse me?"

"You *was* the Second. Here, you're nothing."

Nora raised her chin, trying to hide her nerves. "Am," she said firmly. "I still am. And if you stop trying to—"

The female roared and ran for her again, the male pouncing from the other side.

Ducking, trying not the think about what she was touching as she rolled out of the way, Nora grabbed the small bowl of water and lifted it above her head.

"No!" they both screeched, stilling with hands outstretched.

There was no room in her heart for smugness as Nora witnessed the sheer panic on their faces.

These were the people she had come to this city for. Yes, Aisling had ulterior motives, and yes, Nora had originally planned to escape before arriving, but when everything in Hyrsch had come burning down, this plan had been a phoenix rising from the ashes of her life. A chance to help more demi-kin, to save the imprisoned rebel unit from execution and give them a purpose that would help Aisling for a change. Even if she hadn't been here to see it through, it was an opportunity to do something great.

Being faced with the reality of it had not changed her mind. If anything, she was almost glad she had not escaped the *Airbreaker*.

Slowly, she put the bowl back down on the ground and raised her hands.

"Do you know who Aisling Aurnia is?" she asked.

"Get away from the water, Oford bitch," the female snarled.

These vicious, revolting people were going to be a problem, but Nora knew it was through no fault of their own. Knew it, because she had sat at Owen's side for years, promising it was not his fault when his instincts told him to do something heinous.

She'd taken her revenge on her mother's master years ago, and now she would help Owen take his.

"I'm getting out of here, and I'm going to slit Nevan's throat. You want to be there when I do it? Stop attacking me."

The demi-kin jerked, the female sucking in a deep breath. Then all at once, it rushed out of her in barked, hysterical laughter.

Laughter that went on and on and on.

ARENA

OWEN

Interrupted only by servants who came to relight the torches, the days went by slowly. Until they didn't.

Guards stormed into the holding room, one making a beeline for Owen's cell.

"Somebody's time to shine," Cecelia called from the next cell, making him bristle. Every word out of her mouth drove him batty.

"Face the wall," the guard said, ignoring Cecelia.

Another guard was giving similar instructions to one of the other demi-kin across the room. The male had already been here when Owen and the others arrived and had not uttered a word to them.

Nobody had told them what, exactly, happened in the arena but he doubted both of them would be returning. He understood why the man had not wanted to know him. But now Owen wished he'd at least heard if the demi-kin had fought before or if, like him, this would be his first time. He needed to know what he was up against, because dying now was not something he could afford to do.

Facing the wall, Owen put his hands behind his head. His cell opened and the guard had a knife pointed at his back in seconds.

"Keep your hands to yourself, or lose them."

"Noted," Owen grumbled.

Killing this guard wouldn't get him anywhere, so he didn't resist as a sack was placed over his head, wrists bound tightly in rope before the guard grabbed his elbow and led him out.

He had seen the walls of the arena when they'd first arrived and judging by the cacophony of sound wafting down the hall as the guard led him up, a rowdy audience had gathered for the show.

Owen tuned it all out, needing to focus.

The sun beat down on his sweat-stained shirt, his bare feet burning on the dry sand. Sand. It would slow him down. His weight would be a disadvantage in whatever was to come.

"On your knees," the guard ordered.

Owen obeyed. He couldn't smell past the moldy sack over his head. Couldn't hear anything over the raucous humans high above them.

Breathe, he reminded himself as his heart began to thunder.

His mother had taught him how to breathe. His mother, who had been born in the sewers, never seeing the sun a day in her short, miserable life, but spent her good days teaching Owen how to survive. How to breathe through the festering shit, how to fuel his body on adrenaline and hatred.

Hatred he had not learned to ease until a scar-faced woman had kissed it out of him.

Owen shook thoughts of Nora away. Now was not the time to be distracted.

The hood was pulled away and Owen blinked back the red spots as he adjusted to the daylight.

The first thing he noticed was the shadows. A net had been strung across the arena, separating the demi-kin from the amassed spectators. It left a hatching shadow over the yellow sand, distorting the dips and rises and making it difficult to keep balanced.

Then there was the cage. A narrow, free-standing gibbet, empty with its door wide open, standing atop a wooden platform that had been built in the centre of the arena. After so long training with silver weapons, he recognized the gleam of the bars for what it was. What it likely meant.

The net was not to keep the demi-kin in.

From the opposite side of the arena, a guttural growl resounded behind the locked gate. The quiet male beside Owen began muttering a prayer.

Looking from the gate to the gibbet, from the net to the royal box poignantly empty high above them, it dawned on him what needed to be done.

As the guards jogged for the exit, the wrought iron slamming closed behind them, Owen turned to the male beside him.

"Sorry about this."

"As am I."

A trumpet sounded, the gate across the arena sprang open of its own accord, and Owen jumped to his feet. The other male lunged, knocking Owen down before rolling to his feet and sprinting for the cage.

"Fuck," Owen spat, pulling his bound wrists around to his front before scrambling up.

The beast that prowled into the arena looked like an enormous wolf, except scaled like a lizard, including the fleshy frill around its neck. Battle scarred and half starved, the beast's scythe-curved claws dug into the sand as its piercing gaze tracked the running male.

But it was not stupid. It knew what those bars were made of and set its sights on Owen instead.

"Fuck," he repeated, and ran.

The lupanis sprinted for him.

The other demi-kin reached the cage first, shutting himself inside, holding the bars closed with his bare hands, an apology written on his face as Owen approached.

He had seconds before he'd be reduced to bloody ribbons.

Scrambling up the platform, Owen climbed the gibbet. The crowd was screaming in anticipation as the lupanis closed in, lunging for Owen at the same moment Owen leaped for the net above. He managed to grab hold of the rope, hooking his legs into the netting and pulling his body taut against it, praying it would hold his weight.

Weakened, the lupanis's leap fell short, its claw catching the back of Owen's shirt. The other demi-kin screamed as the beast fell atop the gibbet, echoed by a roar of pain as the heated silver scorched its scales.

The momentum toppled the cage off the platform, and the demi-kin fell out, still clutching the door as it swung open.

Owen didn't see it, but he heard when the lupanis sunk its teeth into the male. Heard the vicious cries of victory from the watching crowd. From where he dangled, he saw money changing hands, smelled the salt and fat of cooked meats being sold from nearby vendors. Some of the humans booed him, throwing stones and rotten fruit at where Owen clung to the ropes.

Where he stayed clinging to them as the lupanis ate its meal.

Even as his muscles screamed with cramps, limbs shaking and stomach churning, he clung to them. Only when the guards released a crossbow bolt into the beast's side and dragged its injured body back beyond the gate did Owen let himself down. Slowly. Ever so slowly, he lowered himself from the net until he hung from his hands, then dropped and rolled on the sand. His ankles complained, his knees barking, but he was mostly intact.

Alive to fight another day.

Drinking deeply, his prize of rotten apples and stale bread in a pile by the cell door, Owen waited for the commentary he knew was coming.

"So, you made it through round one," Cecelia cooed. "How's that escape plan coming along?"

There were moments he could have taken advantage of. Moments that, had he made an attempt to escape, would have ended with a bolt in the skull.

"Tomson," Owen called, ignoring Cecelia.

The general came to the bars of his cell, exhaustion lining his face.

"It can be done," he told him.

Cecelia scoffed.

"Did the spy—"

"Not today." Owen shook his head.

"Why the delay?" Tomson growled.

"Because it could be discovered if they give it to us before Nora and the battalion are ready."

"Assuming Nora is even alive. Assuming anybody is."

Cecelia cackled. "So serious. Though I love the drama. Please, continue."

Owen grimaced, rolling one of his apples across the holding room to Tomson.

Nora was alive. She had to be. Not just because he didn't know what he'd do with himself if she wasn't, but a lot was riding on Nora being able to get close to Rhosyn Shaye.

RHOSYN

NORA

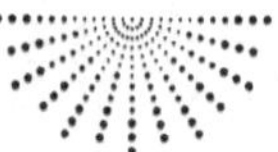

THE BRUSH OF FINGERS AGAINST HER FOOT STARTLED NORA from a shallow sleep. Fists clenched, she swung, but the female sharing her cell scuttled back, hands raised, some kind of beetle pressed between her thumb and index finger.

"Wasn't going to touch you," she croaked, slowly placing the beetle between her teeth. Nora turned away as she crunched down on it.

In the week she had been down in the sewers—or at least she thought it was a week—there had only been food once. It had slid down the trench along the wall, but by the time it got to Nora's cell there was only a handful of raw mince left. Those in the cell on the other side swore and threatened, but the male had taken the lot of it and spat at his neighbors. He had divided the food with the female, both yet to share their names, and ignored Nora's retching.

The water, on the other hand, they shared.

"Meat's no good if you let it rot too soon," the female cackled as she handed Nora the bowl. It had taken longer than she liked to admit to understand that she *was* the meat.

Since then, the water bowl had only filled a quarter of the way again and the lack was wearing her down. There wasn't going to be anything left of her if the spies didn't do their job soon.

The thought of spies conjured images of Siobhan, but wearing the fake nose and wig Nora had found in her rooms, slinking through alleys like a vagrant. Touching her cracked lips, Nora smothered a chuckle. It was ridiculous, and yet it left an oily feeling in her mouth.

The liar. With her pretty dresses and prettier smiles, the infectious laughter, the feel of her soft hands, one on Nora and one on Owen . . .

Then there was that doctor's note.

Nora gagged, closing her eyes.

The crunching of chewed beetle stopped as the other demi-kin stilled, and Nora looked in time to see them backing away from the cell door. It was a few heartbeats before she heard what they had—footsteps, squelching down the hall.

The other prisoners' fear had Nora dragging her tired, heavy body into the corner as well. What little light still emitted from the dying glow worms didn't reach her, and from the shadows she watched three guards stroll past, looking in the door briefly before moving on.

"What's going on?" Nora dared to whisper.

The male had backed the female into the corner, shielding her body with his own, and after a long silence, Nora didn't think she would get an answer. But the male managed to swallow his fear and told her.

"Selection. For the factory."

A shudder ran down her spine and she sagged in relief that their cell had been passed by. But the others were still alert, wide eyes watching the halls.

One of the guards stepped back into view, peering into the darkest corners of the cell.

"This one."

"*Olladista*," the male hissed.

Frowning, it took Nora a moment to realize why the word sent her heart into palpitations. There wasn't much left of the demi-kin language after the Sparrow Coven outlawed it, but that word prickled something deep in her core. A word she had heard whispered in the dark once before, while her mother had thought she was sleeping. Somehow, and at least down here, their ways had not died out yet.

"Say that again and I'll cut your tongue out," the guard spat, fitting a key in the door.

The male seemed prepared to fight, shuffling his feet and balling his fists, but it was Nora the guard looked to.

Scooping a handful of filth from the floor, she prepared to fling it at him.

The door swung open, but none of the guards stepped inside. "I see you hiding in the corner there, Nora Turlough."

The sound of her name was jarring.

"Get up. You're required in the palace."

The other demi-kin flinched, looking to Nora with even wider eyes than before.

It was happening. Finally.

Grunting with effort, Nora got to her shaky legs and tried to wipe her hands clean on her uniform.

"*Ollamiire*," the female whispered.

That was not a word she'd heard, but she gave her a brief nod anyway. Whether they liked or believed her was irrelevant. She would be back for them.

Scrubbed within an inch of her bones and dressed in a crisp white slip, Nora was led through the servants' passages of the palace to a room high up in the turrets. The northern summer sun glared blindingly off the white marble walls and gilded floor, linen drapes fluttering against the open windows. Plush armchairs cloistered around tiny glass tables; four sets spread through the room in a manner Nora had only seen in fancy restaurants back in Hyrsch.

The oversized, elaborately crafted birdcage in the centre of the room suggested that it was not a place for dining, and while the space was by far the most ostentatiously pristine in all of Pirevia, it still reeked of debauchery and blood.

Nora was led by guards to the birdcage, large enough for her to stand in, to pace in, as they locked her in and left her alone.

The light was already giving her a headache, slip growing sticky with sweat as humid heat poured in from the open windows. Her olive skin had gone pale from being underground, and whatever soap they had used in her hair had set her scalp ablaze. Yes, shaving her head had let her flaunt her scars, waving them like a flag of who she was and what she had survived, but the baldness had let her treat the psoriasis plaguing her, too.

Legs shaking, Nora slid down against the bars. She picked at her nails to stop herself from scratching her scalp, but as the doors at the end of the room swung open, the action became a display of false boredom.

Rhosyn Shaye and two of her servants stood before the gilded cage, peering at Nora with cold curiosity.

"She looks hungry."

Despite the hollow, breathy way Rhosyn spoke, the words might as well have been a slap with how hard they hit Nora. Nostrils flaring, she leaned forward as one of the servants brought forward a tray and removed the golden cloche. The human woman wearing a similar white slip to Nora crouched to reveal a bowl of cold porridge before scooping some out with her finger to eat.

Not a taunt, but a test.

Nora waited to see if the servant would react to a poison before snatching the bowl from between the bars.

"What do you want?" she croaked, shoveling a handful of porridge in her mouth.

"That was going to be my question," Rhosyn said, her dimple appearing as she suppressed amusement. "Is it true that you used to be Aisling's Second in Command? That you were kicked out for aiding and abetting rebels?"

"Yes," Nora said between mouthfuls.

Rhosyn narrowed her eyes. "I don't believe you."

Swallowing slowly, Nora met her stare.

As much as she wished otherwise, Nora knew Aisling's interrogation methods and that the princess shared many of them with her brother. She recognized the subtlety of them in Rhosyn's declaration.

"It doesn't matter if you believe me," Nora said. "Because you still haven't answered my question. What do you want, Rhosyn? More than anything in the world, what do you want?"

She had rehearsed this conversation on the *Airbreaker* with

Owen so many times that, even in her half-starved state, she could recite the script.

For a moment, Rhosyn didn't say or do anything. The wheels spinning in her head were almost visible through her translucent blue eyes. But when Nora's insinuation finally registered, those eyes became larger than coins.

Nora finished her porridge and pushed the bowl back toward the servant.

"I can tell you where he is."

"What do you want?" Rhosyn whispered, dropping to her knees and clutching the bars. "Anything. I'll give you anything."

Anything.

She could ask Rhosyn to help her and Owen escape right now. To find one of the other rebels and have them go through with the rest of the plan, promising to send the information about the secret location of Rhosyn's demi-kin lover after the city had fallen.

It had been the plan when she and Owen had attempted to escape the ship. But she was here now, and those demi-kin in the sewer . . . she couldn't leave them behind. Not now that she'd seen them.

"An audience," she said. "With Nevan."

TOMSON

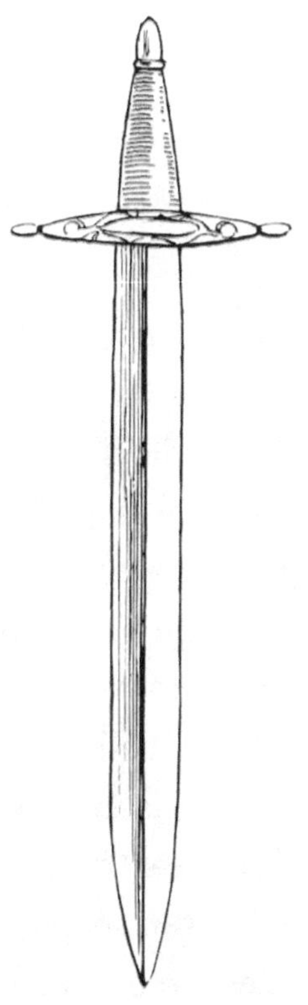

OWEN

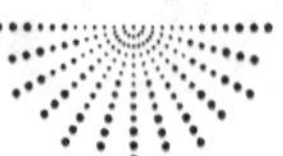

IN THE WEEKS THAT PASSED, ONE OF THE DEMI-KIN REBELS AND two from the royal army who'd come on the *Airbreaker* were taken to the arena and did not return. The rebel had gone with her head held high, but the soldiers . . .

Hearing the plan aboard the ship was one thing, but being in the thick of it now? They were breaking.

Garret had sworn at Owen and Tomson for dragging him into this mess, while Luna had begged and bartered with the guards the whole way down the hall.

"Do all you Hyrschan demis have eels for spines?" Cecelia mocked as Luna's voice disappeared into the tunnel.

"Do you ever shut up?" Owen snapped back.

He and Luna had trained together in the cadets. Had been stationed together outside the palace gates often enough that he knew she preferred liquorice to cream and took her tea with a pinch of peppermint instead of sugar.

The longer it took to get all the pieces of this insurgence into place, the fewer of them there would be to see it through, and Owen was getting nervous.

What in the Mother-made world was taking so long?

The day he finished the last of his food, the guards returned for him. Owen put his face to the wall, hands behind his head again.

"Round two, baby," Cecelia cackled.

He hoped the guards picked her to come with him.

But they didn't. Before they put the hood over his head, he saw them unlocking Tomson's cell.

As he marched up the slope, a string of curses ran through Owen's head. In a fight, he would not win against Tomson. Wasn't sure he even wanted to try.

Tomson was not a rebel in any official capacity, but it had been the general's questioning of Sparrow leadership in Hyrsch that had triggered Owen into searching out the seven-pointed star again. Had sent him to the dank cellar rendezvous where those who didn't believe in the goodness of Princess Aisling gathered. To Edwina and Radley. To Siobhan.

And despite never having affiliated himself with the rebels, Tomson had not hesitated to draw his blade against the Sparrow advisor back in Anfar. There hadn't been a male Owen respected so much since William Copeland and Damien Turlough, and the thought of the Sparrows being responsible for Tomson's death as well hardened the steel edge in Owen's spine.

"Kneel," the guard said, shoving Owen in the sand.

The hood was pulled from his head, his hands unbound for a change. As were Tomson's.

There was no net this time. No gibbet or beast, but a soldier in blue-and-gold armor, a sword at his side. Arms raised in the air, the soldier riled the crowd into some kind of chant.

Owen looked up at them in their finery, holding banners and shouting bets. So much movement and color and sound . . .

There.

Standing at the very edge of the stands was a woman with a seven-pointed star hanging around her neck.

"You see it?" Owen prodded.

"I see it," Tomson said grimly.

The guards left via the wrought-iron gate and a trumpet blew. The Pirevian soldier turned his sword and locked his focus on the demi-kin. He thought he was the hunter, with his fancy armor, polished weapons, and well-fed bulk. Thought the demi-kin were a couple of wild dogs that needed to be put down.

He was about to learn that the demi-kin soldiers of Hyrsch were a different breed entirely.

"You want to lead?" Owen asked.

"Yeah," Tomson muttered, stalking forward, boots sinking in the shifting sand.

Owen grabbed a handful of it, gritting his teeth against the burn of the hot sand on his palm and bare feet.

As they split up, the Pirevian soldier glanced between them, keeping his sword arm closer to Owen but his eyes locked on Tomson. Heart beating so hard he could feel it in his fingertips, Owen let out a wrathful cry and charged. The soldier turned and swung.

Expecting it, Owen skid to his knees and ducked, flinging the sand at the soldier's face. As he reeled, Tomson grabbed a hold of the soldier's wrist. Before he could twist the sword out of his hand, the soldier threw his head back into Tomson's nose. He grabbed hold of the soldier's armor as he stumbled back, dragging him down to the ground with him. Owen lunged for the weapon, but a booted foot connected with his ribs, sending him sprawling.

The crowd screamed as first blood hit the sand, splattering from Tomson's bleeding nose. The soldier swung his sword as he fell, but Tomson was already rolling.

It was harder to get up than Owen expected, his breaths coming too shallow. But he didn't need to breathe. Diving again, he tackled the soldier from behind before the golden-clad witch could get to his feet.

They hit the ground and Owen was close enough to hear the muttering before the ground began to harden. The sand should have made it harder for the soldier to get up, but whatever magic the witch was using had him moving as if solid ground were beneath his feet.

Owen was paying too much attention to the sand.

The pommel of the sword smashed into his jaw, the crack splitting to his temple.

When he opened his eyes again, Tomson and the soldier were a dozen paces away, fist to fist, the sword discarded.

He moved, and his head nearly burst.

The red searing his vision cleared in time to see the soldier get an arm around Tomson's neck, bending him backward until his spine was close to snapping.

Groaning, Owen reached for the sword. It was just out of reach.

Wrapping his hands around the soldier's bicep, clutching his armor for an anchor, Tomson flipped his body, ankles landing over the soldier's shoulders. Locking his feet, he twisted.

The soldier's neck snapped, body crumpling.

Tomson let go, stumbling to his feet and raising his face to the booing crowd. Owen looked to the gates for the guards, but it remained locked. The shouts from the crowd slowly turned back into a chant, but it took a moment for the words to become clear.

"Only one! Only one! Only one!"

Tomson dropped his head and took a deep breath before approaching Owen and collecting the sword. Wincing as he lifted it, Tomson looked down to where Owen was still in too much pain to move his head.

"When you get out of here, give Siobhan my best wishes for the baby. Kiss your wife."

The surprise only lasted a moment. Owen wished he could have brought himself to beg the general to stop. To not do what he very clearly was about to do.

But his mother had taught him to survive.

"It's been an honor, General."

With a grim smile and a knowing look, Tomson raised the sword to his own throat.

"For the seven."

Owen gaped, the words coming with a wheeze. "For the seven."

He did not turn away. Did not let Tomson die alone as the blade opened his throat, a spray of blood washing the sand.

Screams of victory alongside those of shock drowned out the pounding in Owen's ears. The main gates opened and the guards ran in, hoisting Owen to his feet—feet that dragged as the crowd threw things at him. Something soft and sloppy slid down the back of his shirt while a stone cracked against his brow. Something even harder chipped his ear, knocking him to his knees.

"Get up!" the guard shouted, holding Owen under the arm as he fell.

Fumbling through the rotten food under his knees, his fingers brushed against a pointed edge before the guard hauled him back to his feet, shoving him back into the tunnel.

Tossed back in his cell, Owen's head spun and he found himself face down on the ground. The cell door clanged shut behind him and the witch cast whatever spell they used over the lock.

As soon as the guards left, Cecelia's smug face peered through the bars.

"So, how are we feeling about this little escape plan now?" she mocked him.

Owen opened his hand, wiping the blood off the metal seven-pointed charm.

Holding it up, he managed a grim smile.

"Better than ever."

PETER

NORA

WITH WHAT LITTLE TIME SHE COULD GET AWAY FROM THE prince, Rhosyn sat with Nora by the gilded cage. Servants brought a few other meals, mostly porridge and bread, but she was grateful for every morsel. Was grateful to get the chance to read Rhosyn.

The human woman was frightened. That much was evident by the way she continuously wrung her hands as they discussed what had to be done for this plan to work. The bruises that took so much longer to heal on humans than on demi-kin were explanation enough for the nerves. Nora wasn't the only one who'd be in deep shit if this went wrong.

But Rhosyn was also desperate, and that was much easier to manipulate than fear.

It was a sad tale—one that Nevan had bragged about to Aisling at every given opportunity. His pretty human consort, stolen from the demi-kin pirate who'd sacked his merchant ships during a supply run to Dusarn some years ago. Nevan's story about what he'd done to that pirate was always changing, increasing in viciousness every time he told it. Which, Aisling had explained to Nora, was evidence that the torture he described was mere fantasy.

"I know you won't tell me where he is yet," Rhosyn said as she moved to one of the open windows, staring out at the blindingly blue sea crashing against the cliff far below, "but is he okay? Peter?"

Finishing her meal, Nora nodded. One of her tasks this past year had been to track down Rhosyn's pirate. Aisling wanted him as an ace up her sleeve should things ever get out of hand with Nevan. It had been difficult, but she had managed to locate him and had kept a spy on his tail for exactly this kind of opportunity. Ideally, she would have liked to have Peter nearby, waiting, but in the very short period of time she'd been given between Owen's arrest and sentencing to concoct this mad plan, there hadn't been time to correspond.

"Nevan never . . ." Rhosyn's voice was thick as she choked on the prince's name. "He never got his hands on him?"

"No," Nora promised. "He is free."

That was almost more detail than she wanted to give, but the sorrow on the human's face was too close to how she felt whenever Owen had been away from Hyrsch. Inside the city walls they were protected by Aisling's law, but her reign did not extend beyond the city itself; Sparrow law was still enforced by the lords of Oford, and all it would take for Owen to end up back in chains was one of them to be brave enough to try their luck.

Rhosyn sagged, keeping herself upright by her grip on the windowsill alone.

"Do you know why he never came for me?" she whispered.

Carefully, Nora considered how to answer. Admitting she had not actually spoken to him might spook Rhosyn. She might not believe Nora knew where he was after all. To say anything that might suggest he no longer cared for her, or at least not enough to risk his neck, might sabotage her willingness to cooperate.

"He is free," Nora said slowly, "but Nevan hunts him. To come to this city with anything short of an army of his own would be suicide. Gathering one takes time."

It's what she would have wanted to hear had she been in Rhosyn's position. That it was true helped. Coming to Pirevia without an army was suicide, and she hoped the one Aisling promised to send after them would arrive soon.

ESCAPE

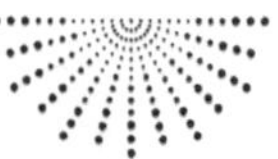

OWEN

HE HADN'T BEEN TAKEN FROM HIS CELL TO FIGHT AGAIN, BUT Cecelia had. Three times. And as she had so smugly declared upon his arrival, she always returned victorious. Battered and bloody, but with enough food to keep her hanging onto this pitiful existence a little longer.

Owen's head had healed enough to let him function, though the headache lingered since his bounty had run out a while ago. Worse though, one of the demi-kin rebels that had been onboard the *Airbreaker* lay in his cell across the room, unmoving. Had been laying there, too still, for almost an entire day. Nobody had called out to ask if he was still alive. They didn't want to know.

"Oh gods, I haven't had mango in forever," Cecelia bragged as she moaned in the cell beside Owen's. The wet slurp of the rotten fruit's flesh as she sucked it clean made his stomach turn.

"I swear, I'm going to kill you," someone else spat, followed by murmurs of agreement.

She only grinned, leaning on the bars of her cell so she could see Owen. "Want some?"

Of course he did. When he reached for the sliver she held out for him, she tutted and pulled it back.

"What's the charm for?"

The silver seven-pointed star pendant lay beneath the nearly empty bucket of water in the corner of his cell. He hadn't explained the details of the plan or the purpose of the charm to the native demi-kin simply because Cecelia annoyed him and he didn't want to give her the satisfaction, but it became a moot point as a tinkling sound echoed from the hallway. A tiny silver ball rolled out of the darkness and into the centre of the room.

Owen grinned, collecting the charm.

"You're about to find out."

Biting his thumb until he drew blood, he rubbed the pad against the metal, feeling the tiny scratches along the surface that some witch had carved. Demi-kin had no magic, obviously, but he'd been instructed by Nora how to activate the charm when it was time. His blood would tie the witch magic to his command, but only for a little while.

As the spellmarks pulsed and the feather-light tickle of magic brushed against his skin, he placed the charm against the cell's lock. Aside from the Sparrow Coven's foul displays, Owen had never seen what magic was capable of. Had never known anyone capable of using it. But as the cell door clicked open, he was grateful that there was at least one witch out there willing to risk the Sparrow Coven's wrath to make this charm for the rebels.

The others watched with wide eyes, rising to their feet as Owen stepped out of his cell. Cecelia lost the smugness, face twisting with rage.

"You were sitting on that the whole time?!"

Ignoring her, Owen collected the silver ball and tucked it into his pocket before heading for the too-still demi-kin's cell first. Opening it, he checked for a pulse, but there wasn't as much as a flutter. Whispering a quiet prayer over the male's body, Owen left him there.

"So," he said, looking around at the desperate faces peering from their cells. "Who's ready to tear this city to the ground?"

HEX

NORA

Still in her gilded cage, Nora stood at the hurried clacking of heels on the marble floor. The door flung open and Rhosyn ran in, flushed and breathless.

"I did it," she panted, closing the door behind her and pulling a golden key from around her neck. "The Hyrschan soldiers arrived outside the gates. I sent the signal."

It was finally happening. Nora's hands trembled as she clutched the bars.

"Did you see them get out?"

"I ran as soon as I rolled the ball down the hall. If any of Nevan's guards saw me . . ."

"No, it's fine. Take me to him."

To Nevan. To end this, and claim Pirevia for Aisling. To set the demi-kin in this city free. To bolster the army they needed in the south.

"Then you'll tell me where Peter is, right?"

Nora nodded. "I swear it."

And she meant it.

Rhosyn unlocked the gilded cage and stood back as Nora climbed down. She hated that all she wore was a white slip, but there would be a sliver of satisfaction in killing the Prince of Pirevia in nothing but a thin dress.

"This way," Rhosyn urged, leading the way to a servants' entrance. "Nobody will ask questions, don't worry. The servants like me."

Weaving through the narrow halls between walls, the servants did indeed lower their heads in a show of respect and step aside as Rhosyn and Nora passed. Perhaps it wasn't a strange sight for them to see the consort hiding among them. Perhaps it wasn't even strange to see her being tailed by a battered-looking stranger with a brown demi-kin mark on the back of their neck. Perhaps Aisling would have more support among the Pirevian humans than expected.

Leaving the servants' passages through a plain door that left them standing outside what had to be Nevan's office, Nora was surprised by how empty and quiet the cavernous hall was. Not even a footstep echoed in the sandstone and marble space, which, considering the lack of rugs to dampen sound, was eerily disconcerting.

Rhosyn knocked on a set of tall, ornate doors and ushered Nora behind her.

A guard from inside the office opened the heavy door and looked the two of them over. Blushing, Rhosyn lowered her gaze and fiddled with the end of the rope that kept her robe closed.

"His Highness asked us to come," she said softly, blinking rapidly, voice quaking.

That the human woman had learned to act such a way made

Nora twist her face into an expression of disgust. Not for Rhosyn, but for the people who had cowed her.

The guard smirked as if this kind of thing happened often. As if Rhosyn's plight amused him. He stepped outside, holding the door to let them by before closing them in.

Sitting at an enormous desk carved from the same marble as the floor, reflecting the sparkling chandeliers high above until the room glittered with gold, was Nevan. Framed by open doors leading onto a balcony, delicate blue drapes fluttering in a breeze that let the odor of his gore-soaked city waft in, he placed the quill in his hand down carefully and folded his dainty pale hands beneath his chin.

Nora couldn't help but stare, the color bleeding from her face. She had heard about the deadly surge in Pirevia, had heard that Nevan was affected by it, but she hadn't expected the marred face staring back at her. Pointed and weaselly with his silver hair tied back, patches of rot had decayed his cheek until teeth and gums were showing. She could see the inner workings of his jaw as he opened his mouth.

"What an unexpected surprise," he said coolly, tilting his head to appraise Nora. "I don't remember giving you permission to bring vermin inside my palace, Rose."

"This is the one I was telling you about," Rhosyn said, sinking to her knees and bowing her head. "Aisling's Second in Command."

Nora stilled, looking down at the consort. They had spoken about her?

There wasn't time to figure out Rhosyn's angle as Nevan stood from his desk. The rot had picked at spots on his neck and arm, too, the rolled-up sleeves of his white silk shirt exposing the blackened wounds.

"Nora Turlough," he said her name like a curse. "As audacious as ever. Though not quite as much so as my sister. This has to be the boldest assassination attempt in the history or Nir."

This wasn't how things were supposed to go, but it didn't matter. Clayton had taught her how to fight. Shifting her feet into position, she loosened her body as much as her aching joints would allow.

"Rose," Nevan called, snapping his fingers before pointing at the floor by his feet. "Come."

The human woman crawled to Nevan, keeping her head down as she resumed her position on her knees. There was shame and regret lacing her features as she refused to meet Nora's eye.

"Tell her the truth," Nevan continued, petting her hair, twisting a strand around his middle finger.

"I told him everything," Rhosyn shuddered. "I had to. He's hexed me."

Nostrils flaring, Nora cursed silently. Their spies had been sure there was no spell—hex, jinx, or curse—on Rhosyn. How they had been so ill informed, she didn't know. Regardless, a hex wouldn't kill Rhosyn, yet even the promise of her demi-kin lover's location hadn't been enough to risk herself.

Nora expelled a sharp breath. It meant that Nevan knew about Owen. About the demi-kin escaping the arena and the soldiers waiting outside the city gates.

As their predicament turned over in her mind, Nevan smiled with the side of his face that wasn't in tatters.

"She recognized you as soon as you got off the ship. The whole time you've been here scheming, I've been preparing. I only fetched you once I was ready to see it all play out."

She should attack. The rapier usually hanging from Nevan's

hip lay across his desk, and Aisling had warned her of the hidden daggers on his person that Nevan would reach for in a pinch. She could best him. She knew it.

But Nevan had not called for his guard. Something about that was nagging at her. He had let her come to him.

"Would you like to see it?" he asked, indicating the open balcony with one of his hidden blades. There was blood on the tip, but Nora forced herself not to look for the source of it.

"See what?" she finally snapped.

The collar around her neck began to burn. Not with heat, but with the bitterly cold fingers of death. Gasping, Nora grabbed a hold of it, trying to break its contact with her skin, but Nevan laughed, raising his hand to show her the bloody spellmark he'd just carved into his palm.

"The plan. Would you like to see the look on your husband's face when it all falls apart?"

SABOTAGE

OWEN

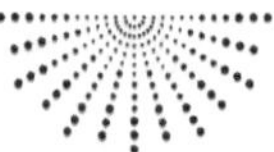

In the dead of night, Owen recognized the cobblestone streets as he led half the freed demi-kin toward the city entrance. The wrought-iron gate in the arena had been left open, no guards waiting outside. A seven-pointed star had been drawn with blood on the wall though, a signal from the spies that they had cleared the way. Cecelia had taken charge of the other half of the group, leading them to the docks. Half of Aisling's army would arrive by ship, the other half via the swamp, leaving no escape for the Pirevians who might flee once the fighting started.

They might have been battered, bruised and half starved, but the promise of Pirevian blood had filled the demi-kin's exhausted bodies with a bristling energy. Owen, too, was finding it hard to sneak along the shadows instead of outright sprinting for the city gates.

Or toward the palace, where Nora was hopefully slitting Nevan's throat.

Every thought in his head was a scream for him to find Nora. Help her. But she was more than capable, and he was needed here.

As the city gates came into view, Owen slowed and held up a hand to stop the demi-kin behind him. They had all found some kind of weapon on the way: loose cobblestones from the road, rusty bits of pipe left in alleys from broken carriages, shards of glass and bent nails. Owen clutched the star pendant, its points sharp between his fingers.

There were four guards inside the gates, likely four outside as well. On either side, towers housing archers with their backs toward the city posed a problem he'd hoped the army might have taken care of before their arrival.

A tap on his shoulder, and Owen turned to see a figure draped in dark fabric standing among the demi-kin, face hidden behind a mask. His eyes dropped to the star pendant around their neck.

Without a word, they nudged past Owen and pulled a blowpipe from within their robes, aiming for the archers. Owen watched as the spy blew out a dart, holding his breath as it sailed through the night and nicked the skin of the archer's neck. He slapped a hand to the wound, but whatever the point was coated with worked quickly, the man sinking to his knees.

Just as quickly, the spy loaded the pipe again and shot the second.

But the guards on the ground had noticed, and as they shouted in alarm the spy ran back into the shadows. Owen raised his chin at the demi-kin.

"To death or glory."

They grinned, then swarmed forward with their pathetic weapons. But rage was powerful, and by the time Owen caught up there was little for him to do. Stealing the sword off one of the guard's bodies, he pressed the charm to the locking mechanism at the gates once more and waited as they rolled open. Four other guards came barrelling through, more prepared than the ones inside, and Owen stepped forward to meet them.

The key difference between a guard and a soldier is that guards are trained to watch and protect, while soldiers like Owen were trained to kill. It was a difference that worked in his favor for once.

He knew the guard would aim for his middle, so he dropped to the ground and rolled into his legs like a bull. Stumbling back, the guard moved to plunge the weapon into Owen, but he stood and rammed his head into the guard's jaw, following it with a jab to the throat with the pointy ends of his steel star as he knocked the guard's blade away.

The man fell, and with the demi-kin keeping the others occupied, Owen stepped beyond the gate to find out why the army had not stepped in to help.

He almost dropped the sword as he looked out across the swamp. Soldiers waited, at least a hundred of them, but clad in blue and gold. Cocky smirks pulled at their mouths as they watched the demi-kin rip apart the guards with amusement. And beside them, along the length of the bridge leading to the distant cliffs, the crimson armored soldiers of Hyrsch lay decapitated in the swamp water, heads on spikes like some kind of sick lampposts.

The soldiers simply stood, waiting for the rest of the demi-kin to notice them. Behind him, Owen heard their sharp breaths. Then their footsteps as most turned away and fled back into the city.

Owen was tempted to raise his sword regardless, but he

could hardly draw breath. His heart had come loose in his chest, sinking into his gut like a lead weight. A single thought remained as the first soldier stepped forward.

Nora.

Every second that passed as Owen fled through the streets, he expected it to be over. For someone to tackle him, shoot him down. But the soldiers only jeered and hollered as they chased him and the other demi-kin, like wild dogs set loose on a hunt. A new plan was forming, rough and impossible. Step one was find Nora. Step two, get down to the dock and steal a boat of some kind.

It would never work. But it had to.

Turning back onto Blood Boulevard, the palace came into view and Owen put on a burst of speed, ignoring the way his lungs burned and knees shook.

What were the chances Nora had managed to kill Nevan? That she would somehow be waiting for him at the palace gates, knowing everything had gone to shit and was ready to run?

A scream behind him sent his heart stumbling, along with his feet, but he didn't look back. The hoots of vicious glee as the soldiers caught someone meant it was too late to help them anyway. Not that Owen would spare a moment to do so. Not with Nora on the line.

Nevan's palace was not as tall as Aisling's, but it was sprawling. Guards stood outside the gates and along the walls with weapons at the ready, but none of them seemed concerned as Owen sprinted toward them.

Of course Nora wasn't there. His eyes scanned the windows

facing the boulevard, spotting three silhouettes standing on a generous balcony on the upper floors. His insides turned to stone as he finally slowed his running. Even with the light behind them and unable to see their faces, Owen would know the shape of Nora anywhere. The sounds of violent merriment were catching up to him, and from the balcony, thunderous laughter echoed its way down to the streets.

Despite it all, he heard Nora's desperate pleading. He'd have heard her from a mile away during a thunderstorm and both his ears full of cotton.

"Owen, run! Please run!"

He could only stand there, shaking his head.

His mother had taught him to survive, but without Nora, he didn't know if he wanted to.

SACRIFICE

OWEN

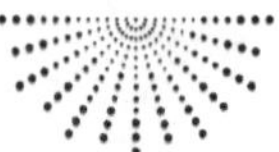

THE DEMI-KIN SAT SILENTLY AS THEY LISTENED TO THE ARENA high above them fill. The noise of the crowd was so clamorous they could hear the excited chatter from all the way down in their cells; bets being placed, refreshments being sold, gossip spreading. No doubt they had been promised a spectacular show today, and Owen had no doubt it would be him.

The footsteps of the guards echoed loudly as they marched down the hall, but Owen didn't open his eyes. A calm had come over him. There were other ways to fight than with violence. His final rebellion would be his refusal to participate.

"Psst."

Owen didn't look.

"Psst, dickhead," Cecelia called.

Things at the docks had apparently gone as well as they had at the gates, but while the demi-kin who'd survived the night and wound up back down in the holding room had cussed Owen out for the failed escape, Cecelia had laughed until dawn.

Owen opened one eye. With her attention on the hall, aware of the oncoming company, Cecelia reached between their cells. In her fingers was a thumb-sized push-dagger.

She knew it would be him, too, and was offering the secret to her success.

Her whole life had been fighting. For Cecelia, there was no other way to go out. Defiance was not in her nature; there was only survival, and she wanted him to have a chance.

"Thank you," he said quietly, taking the push-dagger and hiding it under his armpit.

Perhaps he could follow in Tomson's footsteps rather than engage with whatever nightmare Nevan had concocted.

The guards reached the holding room and did not speak as they unlocked his cell. He did not fight as they led him, unbound and without a hood, back up the hall and into the arena.

The hot sun had baked the ground hard, scalding the soles of his bare feet. The day was too bright to see the crowd properly, but it was impossible to miss that, for once, the royal box was occupied.

Nevan, with his face half covered in a golden mask. Rhosyn, passive and dead-eyed at his feet.

Catching Owen's stare, the prince smirked.

With the guards already behind the wrought-iron gates, the trumpet sounded and the other set across the arena opened. The crowd howled with excitement as Owen took a step back, waiting to see what beast he would face today.

If it was another lupanis, at least his death would be quick, but it was more likely they had rounded up a sandsnake or something equally awful to ensure his suffering would last. At the first sign of that rattling tail, he would use the blade on his own throat.

But neither a lupanis nor a sandsnake came from the monster's den. No, what appeared was far, far worse.

Bare foot in only a white slip, chin raised despite being battered and bruised, Nora stepped into the arena. The gate behind her closed and locked, and the panic crumpling Owen chest was mirrored on his wife's face.

"No," she cried. Walking farther into the arena, turning back to the royal box, Nora shouted over the screaming crowd. "Rhoysn! Please!"

Begging wouldn't achieve anything. Owen knew that. Whatever had gone wrong, it was too late to make it right.

Nevan raised one finger, and the crowd broke into a familiar chant.

"Only one! Only one! Only one!"

Turning his back on the royal box, Owen jogged to his wife and pulled the blade from beneath his arm. One of them had to die.

"No," Nora hissed, grabbing Owen's wrists.

"It's better to do this quick," he told her.

"No!" Her eyes were burning in a way he had once promised they never would again. Not now that they had each other. Not as long as he loved her.

"Whatever they do to you, just hang on," he pleaded. "Aisling will come for you. You know she will."

Nora scanned Owen's face, eyes bloodshot as she slowly shook her head.

Denial was as useful as begging.

"You're going to be a wonderful mother, my sweet Nora."

"Aisling will come," she repeated softly, blinking madly, not truly present. That was probably for the best. He did not envy her the memory of this moment. Of the sacrifice he was about to make.

Forcing a smile, Owen leaned forward to kiss her. He only meant it to be brief, but she pushed closer, hands softening around his wrists to slide up his arms. The crowd whistled and screamed as realization spread of what this slaughter actually meant.

Owen didn't hear any of them. Nora's tears dampened his cheeks as she kissed him harder, cupping his jaw with one hand before pushing it back through his hair, then back down his arms.

Taking both his hands in hers, she pulled back and looked up. "I love you."

"It'll be alright, my love."

"When Aisling comes, tell her I love her too."

Owen frowned. Then his stomach turned over as he realized his hands were empty.

"Nora—"

He grabbed for her as she turned away, reaching for the arm raising the blade she'd stolen. Pulling her against him, panic weakened his knees until they both collapsed to the ground, and he braced himself for a struggle.

Hot red spilled down his arms instead.

"No," he wheezed, lowering her to the ground.

Her throat was open, the blade still lodged in her windpipe despite his grip around her wrist.

"No!"

He pushed a hand against the wound, oblivious to the mixed screams of celebration and disappointment depending on who the Pirevians had put their money on. But denial was pointless. She'd gone too quickly for him to do anything.

Pulling the blade from her neck, he took it to his own. Multiple sets of hands stopped him.

His vision went red.

The screaming of the crowd was indiscernible from the screaming in his head as Owen shoved the hands off and tackled one of the guards to the ground, wrapping a broad hand around his throat before plunging the blade into his eye. A second guard wrapped arms around Owen's chest, trying to pry him off. Owen threw his weight back, toppling the guard and slashing.

Today, Owen was the beast. And nobody was leaving this arena alive.

The unmistakable sound of a sword being pulled from its sheath quickened the blood in his veins. The hot splash of the second guard's blood across his face was permission for Owen to rise, ducking under the swinging sword before kicking the legs out from under the wielder.

"Do not kill him!" Nevan's call was barely audible over the pounding in Owen's ears.

As the guard fell, he stomped on his throat, took the sword, and rammed it into a fourth guard's gut. Spinning around, there didn't seem to be anyone else for him to kill.

Nevan stood at the railing, grinning down at him with a bow in hand, arrow nocked.

Owen didn't care. Switching up his grip on the sword, he had every intention of flinging it at the prince.

The crowd went silent as the prince loosed his arrow and it buried itself in the back of Owen's hand. Cursing, he dropped the blade.

"You know what I'm going to do to your wife's body?" Nevan taunted, lining up a second shot.

With his left hand, Owen picked up the sword. Not to throw

it. He didn't want to hear what the prince was about to say. He didn't want to leave this arena.

The second arrow pierced his left hand and the scream that tore from Owen was as much from frustration as pain. Two more guards strolled into the arena, no weapons bar the smirks on their wicked faces.

"I'm going to carve her up myself," Nevan said slowly, nocking a third arrow. "I'll make a pâté out of her liver. The bones will make a nice broth. I've always found demi-kin steak surprisingly delicious. I'll make a feast out of her, and we will dine together, you and I."

Owen bared his teeth, the threat barely registering.

"Aisling will come."

She would have come, so why, *why*—

But then he knew. There had been a day back when Nora had first taken on the role of Aisling's Second. They had fought. Owen didn't trust the new princess, despite her having freed them. He had told Nora, *"She is still Sparrow. She was born to Sparrows, raised a Sparrow, trained as a Sparrow. She wants to do the right thing, but it is cruelty and wrath that drives her."*

Nora had heard him. And he wished he had never said it.

A third arrow pierced his thigh just as the guards reached him. Owen didn't fight.

To save Nora, Aisling would have come. She would have bartered and sold the world.

But to avenge her . . . Owen could only imagine the kind of destruction Aisling would bring down. So he would wait. Owen would wait for Aisling, and he would do everything in his power to make sure Nevan and his city, his whole fucking coven, burned.

ABOUT THE AUTHOR

 Alex Clifford is an emerging author from the coffee capital: Melbourne, Australia. They have spent the past decade studying creative writing, interior design, sociology, psychology, and secondary education. As a neurodiverse, queer, widowed, single-parent, Alex is excited to bring their unique perspective to the fantasy genre for many years to come. For more on Alex Clifford's upcoming work, visit: www.alexclifford.com.au

You can find her on social media at:
    Facebook: facebook.com/AfsCliffordBooks
    Twitter: @AfsClifford
    Instagram: @almost_alex
    TikTok: @alexcliffordwrites

www.ingramcontent.com/pod-product-compliance
Lightning Source LLC
Chambersburg PA
CBHW020234120726
47903CB00008B/2668